Barty's Ketchup Catastrophe

for Paul

MYRIAD BOOKS LIMITED
35 Bishopsthorpe Road, London SE26 4PA

First published in 1999 by
PICCADILLY PRESS LIMITED
5 Castle Road, London NW1 8PR
www.piccadillypress.co.uk

ISBN 1 904736 69 6

Designed by Louise Millar

Printed in China

Barty's Ketchup Catastrophe

Sally Chambers

MYRIAD BOOKS LIMITED

Barty loved ketchup.
He had it with everything.

He had it for breakfast.

He had it for lunch.

He had it for dinner.

He even had it . . .
for his birthday!

Barty's family thought he was crazy –
"Crazy for ketchup!" they all said.

Barty always had to
help his mum with
the shopping as the
ketchup was heavy.

His friend Cedric hated ketchup. At lunch-time he always brought a peanut butter sandwich for Barty. Barty always put ketchup on it.

One day Cedric invited Barty to a sleep-over at his house. For the first time ever Barty's parents said that he could go.

Barty was really excited.

That day Barty packed and repacked all the things

he would need for his sleep-over at Cedric's.

When he got there he raced up to
Cedric's room and they played

games,

cards

and
puzzles.   Then it was time for dinner . . .

Cedric's family was having one of Barty's favourites – grass pizza!

"Can I have the ketchup, please?"
asked Barty.
"Oh. I don't think we have any,"
said Cedric's mum.

NO KETCHUP!

What a catastrophe!
What was Barty to do?

First of all he watched
everyone else eat.

Then he drank all his drink.

Then he thought he would cry, but he was in Cedric's house.

Finally he thought he would try one little piece.

Then he tried another one and another one.
And then he asked for seconds.
It was quite good really, even if it needed ketchup.

And at breakfast the next morning,
Barty didn't even worry about
not having ketchup for his cereal!

When he got home, everyone thought Barty was cured of his ketchup craze!

But the next time he slept over at Cedric's
there was one thing he didn't forget to pack . . .